CALUM KERR is a writer, editor, Teaching Fellow in Creative Writing at the University of Southampton's Winchester School of Art, and Director of the UK's National Flash Fiction Day. His work has appeared in a number of places—online and in print—and was featured on BBC Radio 4's *iPM* programme. He lives in Southampton with his wife, his stepson, two cats and a dog.

Other books by Calum Kerr

FLASH-FICTION COLLECTIONS

31
Braking Distance
Lost Property

2014 FLASH365 COLLECTIONS

1: *Apocalypse*
2: *The Audacious Adventuress*
3: *The Grandmaster*
4: *Lunch Hour*
5: *Time*
6: *In Conversation with Bob and Jim*

NOVELS

Undead at Heart

TEXT BOOKS

The World in a Flash: How to Write Flash-Fiction

York Notes Advanced: The Kite Runner
York Notes AS & A2: The Kite Runner

Saga

a flash-fiction novella

2014 flash365: volume 7

Calum Kerr

Published by Gumbo Press

First Published 2014 by Gumbo Press.
Printed via CreateSpace.

Gumbo Press
18 Caxton Avenue
Bitterne
Southampton
SO19 5LJ
www.gumbopress.co.uk

A CIP Catalogue record for this book
is available from the British Library

ISBN 978-1502551801

Contents

For my parents,

grandparents

great-grandparents,

great-great-grandparents,

great-great-great-great-great...

and all those without whom.

Family Tree

Happy Birthday, Grandma Dot, love Beth.

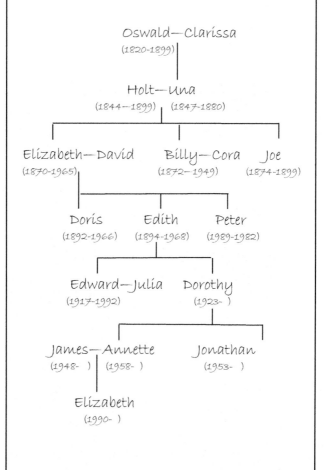

Oswald—Clarissa
(1820-1899)

Holt—Una
(1844—1899) (1847-1880)

Elizabeth—David   Billy—Cora   Joe
(1870-1965)   (1872—1949)   (1874-1899)

Doris   Edith   Peter
(1892-1966)   (1894-1968)   (1989-1982)

Edward—Julia   Dorothy
(1917-1992)   (1923-)

James—Annette   Jonathan
(1948-) (1958-)   (1953-)

Elizabeth
(1990-)

Through the Window

Una waited.

Mother had left for tea with Mrs Rowbotham. The nanny was upstairs, taking care of Una's brother, James.

And Una waited by the window, watching as people moved past, crouched against the rain, the red blood moving through the arteries of the city.

But they were of no interest to her. She paid no heed to the horses on the street, even when one paused to leave an organic gift. She was watching and waiting for one particular figure.

She twisted her handkerchief between her fingers. It was a nervous habit, and Mother had told her not to do it, but she couldn't stop. After all, she *was* nervous.

She raised a hand to her hair, running a hand over it, ensuring the pins were still holding it all in place. She then ran her hand down over her pinafore dress, ensuring it was free of dust or dirt, and was crease free.

She didn't know if he would care, or if he was so used to the dirt from the shop, and from the street, that he wouldn't notice. But she cared. She noticed.

She had stood, unmoving, for over an hour before she saw his head through the crowds. Her heart beat at triple, and then quadruple time, as she made her way, on quick-stepping toes, through to the kitchen.

As was usual at this time in the afternoon, Cook was asleep in her chair by the fire, and Una crept past her to the back door. She opened it, slowly, wincing against the chance of a creak. She stepped out, into the slight shelter of the back porch, and waited, with the door pulled closed behind her.

He came down the lane, and then in through the back yard, and she thought her heart might stop.

He didn't see her at first, his head was down against the weather, and he was concentrating on lifting his feet from the pedals of his bicycle without toppling over. He moved around and pulled a covered basket from the front of the machine, and then turned to the house. Then he saw her, and stopped.

She felt her eyes widen as his gaze met hers, and for a moment she thought he was going to bolt.

She gave him the smile she used on nervous puppies, and beckoned him forward.

He did so, seeming to gain confidence with each step.

When he reached her, he had regained his height and his bearing. He smiled back at her, and she felt herself flush.

He reached into the basket and produced two loaves of bread.

"Is this for you, miss?" he asked.

She nodded, suddenly shy, and took the loaves from him.

"Thank you," she said.

The boy turned to leave, and then turned back. "My name is Holt," he told her.

"Una," she said, her voice little more than a squeak.

"Very pleased to meet you, Miss Una," he said. "Same time tomorrow?"

She nodded, feeling something warm kindle within her.

Family

It is still dark when I rise from my bed, though that is nothing new. The work in the bakery was largely carried out during the hours of darkness, so this new post as a clerk feels little different.

The others I work with do not have to rise so early, but they do not have to practise their letters and numbers as I do. They do not have to read and reread to understand their instructions. They do not have the fear of disappointing their father in law, known to them as their manager, Mr Greer, to disturb their slumber.

I tell none of this to Una of course. She knows I rise early to prepare myself for work, but she doesn't know the emotions which drive me. I have to do well. I have to prove that I can do this – to her father and to myself. I can't let her down, not after everything she has given up for me.

But each morning, like this one, when I rise I don't immediately light a candle and settle down to work. Each morning, I pause, and in the dim light which filters through the windows, I carry out the same benediction.

Dressed, I move back to the bed and kneel at the side, as though in prayer. I do not bow my head, however. Instead I face forwards and I look at her: my wife.

She does not know I watch her sleep, but I cannot help myself. Her beauty is eternal, but at this time of day, when she is completely at rest she is, if anything, even more beautiful. She lies, her hair spread across the pillow around her, her proud profile lifted from its darkness. Below that, the blankets swell to cover her body, whose form I know so well. Each swell of hip or breast is ingrained in my memory, and in my mind I kiss every inch of her skin.

Today, however, is slightly different. Today is the first day that one can notice the difference, and rather than merely paying my respects at the altar of her exquisite form, I reach out my hand.

I place it gently on the extra swell of her body, and think of the new life within. For a moment my thoughts move forward in time, attempting to imagine the future that this new life will know, and imagining the generations beyond.

But then I regather myself and rise. There is no time for speculation. It is time to redouble my work. It is no longer my father, my wife and myself that I can let down if I do not become the best of men. Now there is another, still more precious, and I must get to work.

When the Time comes

Mother says that I will have to look after everyone after she's gone. She says that I will have to do the things that she does and be a good mother to Billy and Joe. She says that I will have to take care of Daddy and make sure he is fed and that he sleeps.

He doesn't sleep very much. I know because sometimes I wake up, and it's night and very dark, and he is awake, sitting with a single candle, reading his papers.

We don't have to use candles most of the time. We have gas lights. They aren't as bright as daylight, and they flicker and they smell funny, but Daddy says they are a sign that we are living in the future.

He says that means that things are changing, and that we can never stop them changing, and that I will be alive when the century changes and will actually see the future arrive. He says everything will be better in the future.

I don't know about that, because Mother says that in the future she won't be around to care for us, and that doesn't sound better to me.

She says it's not yet. She was ill and coughed a lot,

but she's better now. But she says it will come back and then it will not go away and eventually it will consume her. No-one knows how to make it stop, and eventually it will mean that she isn't here anymore.

I sit on her knee, and she helps me to read, and then she tells me about the things I will have to do when she is gone. She tells me how to clean, and how to cook. She has shown me how to change little Joe's nappy, and she says that I am very good.

She says that she is very proud of me, and she knows that when the time comes, I will do a wonderful job.

It makes me happy when she says that, but I just wish that she would stay.

Goodbye

The rain fell, the music played, and the bearers walked slowly, carrying the coffin into the church.

Holt stood and watched with his children around him, attempting to shelter them all under a single umbrella, and his lids scraped across hot, dry eyes.

They followed into the chapel and took their seats at the front. Elizabeth organised her brothers and made them sit nicely. They didn't require much instruction. They were too subdued by the whole experience.

Holt wondered if it had been easier on them if Una had died when she first fell ill. Would it have been better if they had been too young to know what had happened; to understand what they had lost?

He thought maybe it would have eased their distress, but not for a single moment would he take away from them everything Una had been able to bestow. She had been a steady light in a dark world, and despite the pallor cast by her passing, she would banish their shadows for the rest of their lives.

He sat through the service, stood when he needed to, mouthed the words to the hymns and made the responses required of him, but he was not present. He was living – reliving – a life which had been rich but all too short.

He had not been asked to deliver the eulogy, and for that he was glad. He was unsure whether his legs would have carried him to the lectern or his voice carried his thoughts to the congregation.

Her father, his employer, undertook that duty. He spoke of a daughter, and of love, but Holt sank into his memories and spoke words private to him which the father could never understand.

At the end of the service Elizabeth, organising him now, as well as her younger siblings, led them to the rear of the church where, by rote, he thanked all those who had attended, to pay their respects to his dead love.

The last, by design Holt was sure, was Una's father, Oswald.

He paused in front of his son-in-law and gave a slow nod to Holt's litany of gratitude, and then he placed a hand on the younger man's shoulder and turned them so their backs were to his grandchildren and the few lingering mourners.

He spoke in a low voice, but there was no mistaking the vehemence. "I never wanted her to be wasted on one such as you. I told her not to marry you, and see – with your life you have killed her. You have taken away my beloved daughter and I will never forgive you. I would cut you off without a penny, dismiss you from my employ, and feel satisfaction as you expired in some poor house. But, for the sake of the children, the last remaining vestige of the beauty you have ruined, I will not do so."

Holt listened in silence. This was not unexpected. These were accusations he had also levelled.

"But, be warned, you are on notice. First and foremost, they are not your children. They are mine. And if I so choose they will be taken from you and you will be cast aside. Do we have an understanding?"

Holt nodded and, with a long hard squeeze, he was released.

Oswald turned, ignoring the children he professed such affection for, and walked away.

Holt looked down and met Elizabeth's eyes. She had her mother's face, and for a moment he felt a sob attempt to rise in his throat. He could tell from her expression that she had heard Oswald's words to him, and her face contained a deep anger.

She gave a long, slow nod, and then reached up to take her father's hand.

A Different Waiting Game

She sat in the deep recess of the window and read her book. She was the very model of decorum. A studious pupil, every hour that she did not spend at school, or helping the nanny with her brothers – mostly cleaning them up after another session of rough and tumble – she spent reading books.

They mesmerised her. Each cover was a doorway to another, better, world. Even if they were grim or frightening, they were better worlds because they were not this one.

However, today she could not lose herself. Yes, she was a model of decorum, but only a model: a facsimile. She feigned her posture and her attention on the book, while her gaze flicked from the page to the world on the other side of the glass and back again. She feigned because she could not openly watch. Grandfather would not approve.

Her fingers were damp on the pages of the book, causing them to soften and wrinkle in her grasp, but despite her usual fastidiousness, she did not care. She had glimpsed him yesterday, and she hoped, if she waited, that she would see him again.

She had sat for over an hour, and it was starting to grow dark. The lamps were being lit, guttering in their shades. He appeared under one of them, no more than a shadow at first, but then he stepped forward and her heart gave a double beat as she saw his face.

She slid from her seat and gave a silent prayer that she would not be interrupted, and then made her way through the kitchen to the back door.

Cook was asleep in the kitchen and she stole past, opening the door with care to avoid a creak, and stepped out onto the back porch, pulling it shut behind her.

He crept along the back alleyway, keeping to the shadows, and for a moment she wanted to cry. But she held it back, steeled herself. She was stronger than this.

Finally he was in front of her.

Her father was thinner than when she last saw him, but he seemed to be clean.

"How are you?" he asked.

"Well, thank you. Grandfather does not mistreat us."

He nodded. "And the boys?"

"Are boys," she replied.

His lips curled in a slight smile, and Elizabeth felt the tears make another attempt. Again she fought them back.

"And how are you?" she asked him.

He gave a small nod. "I am better for seeing you. But in truth it has been hard. I am still far from able to bring you home."

She nodded, biting her lip, then reached into the deep pocket of her pinafore. She extended her hand and he took the half loaf of bread from her with murmured thanks.

However, when she tried to press a handful of shillings upon him he refused.

She tried again, but he curled his hand around hers and pressed it back upon her.

"No, little Lizzie. That is yours. You need it. Use it for something special, something your mother would have bought for you if she were here."

"I miss her."

"I miss her too. And I miss you."

The tears came then, and Elizabeth could do nothing to stop them. She leaned forward and let them run out onto her father's jacket while he held her, and then he gripped her shoulders and straightened her.

"Be patient, my girl," he told her. "All will be well in the end."

"Are you sure?"

He nodded, a firm and confident gesture, and placed a kiss on her forehead. Then he turned and left. He did not say goodbye.

The Biggest Day

"Can you leave me for a moment, I wish a little peace?" Elizabeth spoke in a low voice, but the tone was not to be disobeyed. Enid, who had been straightening the edge of the dress, stood up, kissed her friend on the cheek, and left.

Oswald shifted from foot to foot, looking around the small ante-chamber which served the dual purpose of clergy-robing and bride-waiting. Elizabeth looked at him with a frank gaze which the import of the day allowed her, and raised an eyebrow. He touched a hand to his chest. "You wish me to leave too?" he asked.

She stepped up to him and kissed his cheek. "Yes, please, Grandfather. I just wish a moment to gather myself."

"David is a good man, you know?"

She smiled. "I know. I know he is. I just want a moment before I have to be in front of so many people."

Oswald nodded. "Yes, of course," he said, and followed Enid. He closed the door gently behind him, and Elizabeth turned to face the slim robing-mirror on the wall.

She took a deep breath and held it, then released it through her nose, feeling the erratic beating of her heart start to slow.

"All is well," she whispered to herself. "All will be well."

"And all manner of things will be well?" said a voice behind her. Elizabeth gasped and turned, her hands rising to cover her mouth and stifle a scream as a figure emerged from behind a rack of cassocks.

As she recognised him, her hands dropped. "Father!"

"My darling girl," said the man, stepping forward and taking her hands.

He was unrecognisable from the last time she had seen him. His skin was pink and plump, his hair and whiskers well groomed. His suit was well-tailored and immaculate, his shoes were buffed to a high sheen, and a gold watch chain glimmered from between the leaves of his coat.

"I told you, didn't I?" he said.

She nodded, feeling tears spring from her eyes.

"I told you I would better my prospects and I would be back."

Again, she nodded, smiling widely even as the tears flowed down over cheek and chin.

"And what better day could there be?"

Her eyes widened and she glanced to the door. "Does Grandfather know?"

Holt shook his head. "Not yet. But he will soon," he said and extended his crooked arm. "Ready to take a walk?"

Elizabeth smiled at him, and felt her heart finally grow calm. "Yes," she said. "I am."

Leaving Home Isn't Easy

"But I don't understand. Why can't you just work for Father, like Billy? Why do you have to go and do this?"

Joe shrugged. "Sorry, Lizzie. It's what I want to do. I'm twenty-one now, remember. I get to make my own choices and be my own man."

Elizabeth brushed a loose lock of hair out of her eyes and fixed her younger brother with her sternest glare. He laughed.

"You can stop that, my beloved sister. That look might have worked when we were small, and it might work with your little ones, but I'm afraid it doesn't work on me anymore."

She gave an annoyed grunt. "Because you are twenty-one, I suppose?"

Joe gave another laugh and held his arms out from his sides in proof of his status as an adult.

The gesture wasn't really necessary. The uniform he was wearing was proof enough of his coming of age. It was a dull, dusty green, and seemed to be too large for his slender frame.

"I thought they were red," Elizabeth said after a

moment's thought. "The redcoats."

Joe shrugged and gave his sister a little twirl. "They were. They're not now," he said.

"What do they call that?"

"Khaki, apparently."

"What kind of a word is that?"

"Indian."

"Oh. India. Is that where you're going?"

Joe shrugged. "Dunno, sis. I'll go where they send me. But they're going to train me first."

For a moment his smile faltered, and Elizabeth saw the fear he was hiding. Almost without transition she was standing and wrapping her arms around him.

"Don't go, little brother. Please." She buried her face in his neck.

Joe hugged her back, hard, and then disentangled himself.

"I have to," he said. "I have to."

Fin de Siècle

I should be readying myself for a celebration this evening. David has invited his cousins for dinner and drinks to see in the arrival of the new century. I cannot, yet, however, find my way to a frame of mind which will allow me to be merry with company. The last months have been hard, too hard to write here, but I feel I need to put down in print all of my thoughts before I can move on to a new phase.

Christmas was a subdued affair, with just myself, David, Doris, Edith and Peter. The children enjoyed themselves. I did not.

Reading back, my last entry talked about my worries about Joe and the new war in the Transvaal. We had just heard the news of the outbreak of hostilities, but what I didn't know is that Joe was already dead. He died on the second day of the siege, when his position was hit by shells.

We received word two weeks later, but I had

already stopped writing because we were already dealing with death.

My father, Holt, died on the twenty third of October. He was fifty-four years old. He was at work, and his heart stopped. There was nothing we could do, nothing we could have done. It was just his time, but that did not make it any easier to accept.

With Oswald dying in June, it has left me feeling as though the oncoming century is some kind of harbinger. I just do not know what it's bringing.

Sometimes, I think it is bringing progress, advancement, a world which would not be fit for men such as my father and grandfather. A world in which they would not fit, and so they had to leave before it arrived.

But another part of me – the part which died when little Joe did – fears that it is bringing pain and death. I worry that the trials and tribulations of the past hundred years – the death, the poverty, the war – have been an overture to a larger cataclysm.

And so I wonder, how can I go downstairs and celebrate the arrival of this new epoch that rides on a pale horse?

And yet...

And yet I must.

If there is one thing I have learned from the men in my life who have passed – from the obstinacy of my grandfather, the perseverance of my father, and the optimism and dedication of my brother – it is that each day you must wake up and tackle whatever faces you. That is the only way to live your life, because you can never know what will happen next.

And so, I suppose, writing this all down has been largely pointless. For I shall rise now, ensure my dress and appearance are appropriate for the company, and I shall face whatever comes when midnight arrives and eighteen becomes nineteen.

It is the only way.

Hot

So much is different here. The streets, the buildings, the plants and animals. The people.

And it's hot.

It's hot all the time. I knew it would be, but the reality...

My sister told me to expect it – she's always looked after me – but even she couldn't imagine what it's really like. It's so different to England.

And Sydney is such a young city. You can feel the life springing from its cobbles.

I don't live in the city. I came here to get away from that. After Father... well... I needed space. And that's something you can find here in abundance.

I live outside of the city, on a farm. Father's money, and Grandfather's, have allowed me to travel and to buy the house and the land. I don't need to farm.

But from time to time, like today, I have to come into the city. I need the people, the bustle, the crowds.

It's so different. I wish Lizzie could see it. And

feel the heat.

It's hot. So hot.

From the main street I walk into a darkened alleyway. It's cooler down here, and dimmer.

In the dirt, I notice a glimmer. When I bend down, I see it's a shilling. An English shilling. It's a few years old, and has a picture of the old Queen on it, but it still has a shine to it.

I crouch there, in the darkness of this Sydney alleyway, and I turn the coin over in my hands. It gives me a pang.

Home seems so far away, and so long ago. It's only been a year, but this is really a new world.

I stand up and pop the shilling in my pocket. It's worthless here, but maybe one day I will have a chance to spend it.

I'll show it to Cora. I don't know if she has ever seen one.

My Generation

Mother just doesn't seem to understand. It's a new world, a new century, a new decade and she just doesn't have the ability to grasp what it is like to be a young woman at a time like this.

I told her, last night, "It's nineteen-ten, not eighteen-eighty. Everything's changed. A woman can be free and can do what she likes now."

"Can you vote?" she asked me, and Father gave a small smile into his tea. It was good that Mother didn't see him. She wouldn't have been amused, and she would have told him so.

I try to tell her that I'm taking after her. She's so strong, is Mother, so forthright in her views. Why shouldn't I be the same? Why shouldn't I be allowed to do what I want, and go where I want, and see whomever I want? After all, we have the money.

"That's beside the point, Doris," she said to me when I said this. "I grew up with little or no spare money in the family. Even after my mother died and Grandfather Oswald took us in, while we lived well, we were given little to spend. And you know that your father and I have had to struggle at times."

I presume that was what she said, and probably more, but I have heard it so many times before that it all becomes like the grey noise you hear if you hold a shell to your ear. Some people tell me it is the sound of the sea, but I think it's just the echo of sound in a small enclosed chamber. I didn't say that, of course, I stood like the dutiful daughter and waited until the end of her speech.

Patience is ever the key.

"I know, Mother, and it must have been terrible," I told her when I realised that she had finished. "But I am eighteen years old now. It is no longer the nineteenth century, we are no longer poor, and all I would like is to go to one dance."

Mother looked angry, but I would swear that I saw a hidden smile curl the edge of her mouth. "It is not just a dance it is a ball. Is that how you see yourself? The little debutante?"

I said nothing, just waited. This was the crucial moment.

Father's newspaper rattled as he settled it to his lap.

"It's been a while since we have been to a ball, Elizabeth. There might be no harm in our going and introducing Doris to some of our friends."

Mother looked at him and then back at me.

"Very well. But you stay with us, and you come home with us when we tell you to. And you do what you're told all the time we're there."

I ran over and kissed her on the cheek. "Yes, Mother. Of course, Mother. Thank you, Mother."

I did the same with Father, but slightly more soberly. I know he doesn't like fuss.

Of course, I would have liked to go on my own, but I knew that was highly unlikely. Still, I can't wait to be there.

There will be boys.

Work

"It's not right, that's all I'm saying."

David sighed and sat back in his chair. Lizzie had walked in and started talking as though they were in the middle of a conversation and, he supposed, in a way, they were. It was an argument which had been going on for months now, and he doubted it would stop. It was tiring.

He raised his eyebrows, knowing that she didn't need any more prompting than that.

"She should be up here with me and Edith. Or at least in the typing pool."

He nodded. It was true. When the call had gone out for women to go into work to take the place of men sent off to war, he had envisaged his wife and daughters coming to the office with him every day. He saw shared lunches and some, careful, laughter.

But that had not been enough for Doris. She wanted to show the world. She wanted men to know that women were as good as they. And so she worked down on the factory floor with the men, ensuring she did at least as good a job, at least as long a shift, at least as much hard labour as they did. What Doris wanted, Doris got. It had always been the way.

But Lizzie hated it. She admitted the need to help the war effort – while keeping a close eye and a firm grasp on Peter, who was only one year away from being old enough to enlist – but she didn't see why her eldest daughter needed to put herself in danger working with metal and fire and explosives.

David wished he had an answer, but women were and had always been a mystery to him. It was safer to say nothing and wait to see what happened.

"Can you not go and have a word with her?"

He didn't see how it would help. It hadn't had any effect the dozens of times he'd tried before. But Lizzie was so like her daughter, even if she didn't want to admit it. What Lizzie wanted, Lizzie got.

He shrugged and stood up from behind his desk.

As he walked through the office door – which Lizzie had left open so the rest of the secretaries could hear all that had been said – there came a muffled explosion from downstairs.

David wasn't aware of his actions, he just ran and moments later he was on the main floor, pushing through a knot of workers.

Between bodies he saw the red scarf which Doris insisted upon wearing, and for a moment he feared his heart would seize in his chest. He let out a low cry and barged forward into the ring of space at the centre.

His breath emerged in a whoosh when he saw

that Doris was unharmed. She was kneeling next to a man who was clearly dead. Where his forearm had been was now a blackened stump, and half of his face was missing.

Doris looked up at him, tears cutting clean lines through the soot on her face, and David knew that while Lizzie would now be even more determined to bring her daughter up to the safety of the offices, Doris would be even more determined to stay.

The Burning

He stood and watched the city burn and felt empty. His colleagues, most of them, were cheerful, and thought nothing of taking aim at the firefighters attempting to tackle the blaze, but although his rifle was up, and his finger was moving on the trigger, Peter was careful to aim low, away from the men, aiming to miss.

It had all seemed so simple before. In the trenches, or back in the barracks, he had known why he was there. An enemy needed defeating before it swamped Europe and ended freedom. That much he had been able to understand, even if his mother hadn't.

And then, signing up for more duty, more defence of freedom – even in a khaki uniform which had been mixed with a threatening black – had seemed like the obvious thing. He was not ready for the real world, for civilian life. The army was all he knew, and he was proud to be a part of it like his uncle before him.

But being here, fighting this foe, it felt wrong.

These were people like him. Yes, they spoke

Irish, but they also spoke English. He had fought alongside some of them in Belgium and France. They lived in houses he recognised and, as far as he knew, they just wanted their country to themselves. Why was he here? What was this all about?

His rifle empty, he dropped behind the barricade to reload and looked around. Tommy and Bill were still firing, grins on their faces. Patrick dropped down next to him, reaching for more bullets, and let loose a laugh. "Like fish in a barrel," he said and bent his head to his task.

Peter responded with a fake laugh of his own.

"If only the Hun had been so obliging," he said, and felt ashamed of himself. He knew he had to fit in, but day by day it was making him feel sicker and sicker.

He looked down at his boots as he loaded his gun, wondering how much it would hurt if he put a bullet through one of them, then raised himself back to the vantage and took aim, once more, at the patch of dirt which lay between him and the 'enemy'.

A Visit

She watched him walk down from the ship, and shifted Dorothy in her arms. Edward ran around her legs in endless circles which she knew would end with him collapsing to the floor, shouting about dizziness.

She knew what Uncle Billy looked like from her mother's old photographs, but she hadn't been prepared for how much he looked like Mother.

"Edith?" he asked as he approached.

She smiled, shifted the baby and held out a hand.

"You look just like our Elizabeth," he said, as he shook it, and she laughed.

He gave her a quizzical look, but she shook her head.

"This is Cora," he said, indicating the woman standing behind him. She was tall and dark, which was not what Edith had expected from an Australian, though her tanned skin looked right.

"Good to meet you," she said, and shook Edith's hand with a strength the younger woman wasn't expecting. Her accent sounded strange to

Edith's ears, but she found herself warming to the woman anyway.

"This way," she said and turned to lead them towards the station.

Edward, who had been hiding behind his mother's skirts, now stepped out and walked alongside the visitors.

"I'm Edward," he said.

"Pleased to meet you, Edward," said Billy.

"I'm eight," said Edward.

"Well done," said Cora and the boy giggled. He ran around the two of them, then slipped in between then and reached up to take their hands.

"How long has it been?" asked Edith.

"Nearly twenty five years," replied Billy.

Edith glanced at him in surprise. "Really? Has it changed much?"

Billy laughed. "England? I don't know. I haven't seen any of it yet."

Edith blushed and ducked her head, and Billy gave a small laugh which Cora echoed. Edward gave a cackle, though it was clear he hadn't been paying attention. He pulled away and ran ahead.

"But, if the rest of the world is anything to go by," Billy continued, "then it will have changed and it will have stayed completely the same."

"Is that meant to be wisdom?" Cora asked him.

"As close as I can get," Billy said and gave a loud laugh. Dorothy gave a little squawk, but Edith shushed her.

"Just you today, then?" he asked, after a moment.

Edith nodded, and guided them through the door into the waiting room of the station. "The next train is due in about twenty minutes," she said and they sat down with Cora and Billy on either side of her and Edward doing laps of the room. "And, yes, just me. Doris is off campaigning somewhere, and Peter is... well. And Father's at work and Mother is just getting over a cold. So, yes, sorry, just me,"

Cora turned to her. "Hey, don't be down on yourself. We were just wondering. Campaigning, you say?"

Edith nodded, blushing again, but with a pleased smile on her lips. "Yes. She wants to be a Member of Parliament."

Billy laughed. "Now that sounds about right. I think our Lizzie would have gone for that if she could."

"I'm going to be a train driver!" Edward shouted as he came to sudden halt in front of them, panting. He then rushed off again, this time chuffing like a train.

"So, how long are you visiting," Edith asked, looking up at the clock.

Billy and Cora exchanged a glance which Edith didn't understand.

"Not sure, yet," he said. "We'll see."

"I'm going to be a train!" Edward shouted from the far end of the room.

Another Visit

"Don't go, then. It makes you too distressed. For days. It's not good for you."

It was the usual discussion. David never wanted me to go, but I always went anyway. His argument was true. It does hurt me to see him. But what David doesn't understand is that the visits are not about me. Whatever they might do to me, my visits are for Peter's good, not mine. They are just one of the possible burdens you accept when you create a life.

The hospital is an hour's drive away. That is both a blessing and a curse. It is close enough that I visit him often, but far enough away that I don't feel I have to go every day.

But it's also far enough away that I have time to wonder how he will be when I get there. Sometimes it is long enough for me to get my hopes up. Sometimes it is long enough for me to dread what I will find. Always, on the way back, it is long enough for the tears to dry on my face so that David never really knows the full effect the visits have on me.

He had asked me, a few times, if I want him to come with me. But I have always said no. I think he worries about me driving, but I'm only sixty, I'm not dead yet. And I know he worries about how they make me feel. But I also know that he would not cope even as well as I do.

I think the countryside around the hospital is probably good for Peter, but I can't really tell.

He doesn't look up as I walk into the ward. He never does.

I sit down on the chair next to his bed and take his hand in mine. It is slack, with no attempt to grip. If it wasn't for his eyes being open, I would think he was dead or in a coma, but his eyes move and flicker as though he was watching a film being shown on the far side of the room.

When he is thirsty he drinks. When he is hungry he eats. Sometimes I help to feed him.

He never speaks.

I'm still not sure what happened to him in Ireland with the Black and Tans. No one would tell me. But whatever it was it left him like this.

And now, once a week, I visit him. Once a week for nearly ten years I have sat and held his hand. I tell him about Edith and the children. I tell him about Doris and her one-woman crusade for world domination. I tell him about Billy and Cora and their cottage. I tell him everything, hoping that one of my words, dangled like a hook in front of him, will prove enough to reel him back up from whatever depths he finds himself in.

Afterwards, I come home, and I wait another week. I talk, I listen, I live my life, and I wait.

Sisters

- So, how is it all coming along?

- So far, so good. The election is in just over two weeks, and I think I might finally have a chance of winning a seat.

- That would be so marvellous. I can't imagine my sister might be a Member of Parliament.

- It has been a long journey.

- How long now?

- Well, since I started trying to run, it's been ten years. But you know I've wanted this ever since… well, ever since.

- That's true. Am I remembering it right? Did you used to make me take part in ballots about what games we would play, what treats we would ask for?

- Oh, I'd forgotten that. Yes. Ha. Yes. I did. Oh, I'm sorry. I'm so sorry for that.

- Don't be. It's funny. It's something I can tell people when you become Prime Minister.

- Ah, now who is being funny? There will never be a woman Prime Minister. Not for hundreds of years.

- Don't be so sure, Dor. Look at what's happened

in just the last thirty years. Thirty more, and who knows?

- I suppose. I guess anything's possible.

- Of course it is. Including the fact that you are going to become an MP two weeks on Thursday.

- Thanks, Edie. You've always been a good support. Anyway, what about you. How are the children?

- Oh, they're very well. Edward's finishing school. He's talking about going to university.

- Really? He would be the first, wouldn't he?

- He would. I'd be so proud.

- And is Dotty still adorable?

- Oh yes, of course. She sends her love to her favourite auntie.

- Her only auntie.

- I try not to mention that.

- Thank you.

- Have you been to see Peter recently?

- Not since Christmas. I feel awful about it.

- Me too. But there's nothing to do about it.

- Does Mum still go?

- Every week.

- I don't know how she does it.

- Nor me.

- She's quite amazing.

- She is, she is.

- But she raised two pretty amazing daughters too.

- Agreed.

- More tea?

1940

The air under the wings became a solid support, allowing the plane to glide and soar, and for a few moments Eddie could forget why he was up here. He could pretend that the bullets would not stream towards him, that the shells and flak would not burst around him, that the ground did not have the ability to come far too close far too quick. He could enjoy the sky, and the freedom, he could feel the controls responding to his touch and believe that all would be well. It was the best part of his day.

"Yes, Mum," Peter said when Lizzie asked him if he wanted a cup of tea. The hospital had sent him home. His bed, his ward, was needed for the new influx of servicemen. At first Lizzie, and David, now in their seventies, had found it all too much. Edie had moved in with them to take care of her brother. But something about being at home had brought him back from whatever world he had been stuck in. When he spoke his first words,

Lizzie sank to her knees and buried her face in the blanket which swaddled his knees, and cried.

Billy sat and read through the instructions again, trying to understand what the various coupons meant, trying to work out how he was going to feed himself. He thought about his garden and wondered if his back would remain strong enough to allow him to dig for victory. He wondered what use his money might be. He wondered how he was still alive when he had lost all that was precious to him and the world had gone mad.

Doris rose to her feet in the council chambers. They needed to listen. They needed to understand. They needed to change and adapt and prepare for a war which had not been over by Christmas. She knew she had her work cut out for her. They were men; old men. They believed they knew what was going on. But they needed to listen, they needed to be told, and that was her job.

Dorothy lay on her bed and stared at the ceiling. She wondered about her brother, and hoped he was okay. And then she thought about the other young men who had been called up with him. She thought about watching them, in their uniforms. She wondered what they would be like when they came home. She wondered if they would like her. She wondered if she would find one to marry. She wondered what her husband would look like. She wondered what her wedding night would be like and her breathing quickened.

The words 'Battle of Britain' drifted through Eddie's mind, Churchill's voice spurring him on. This was the fight. This was the chance to protect his country, his life, his family. He heard the orders over the radio, looked around for his comrades, and prepared to engage.

Victory

They had known that the news was coming. The last days had seen event after event, each leading in an inexorable direction. But still, like most, they waited for the official word.

"Why the Americans?" asked Elizabeth, but no-one minded her. They just kept listening as the announcement rolled on, and as they realised that it was finally true, that the war was finally over, they cheered and embraced.

Edie pulled Peter up from his chair and he held onto her and sobbed, letting go.

Doris crouched down next to Uncle Billy and put her arms around his neck. He hugged her back and then let out a roar akin to a battle cry.

David reached out a hand along the sofa to his wife, and she took it and held it firm. A single tear ran down her cheek.

Dorothy was sitting on the floor next to her grandparents, watching the celebrations. She craned her neck to look up at her grandmother.

"Are you happy, Gran?" she asked.

Elizabeth looked down at the girl, and tried to

remember what it was like to be so young, and to feel things in a way which was so strong, and so uncomplicated.

"Of course I am, love," she said.

"Eddie made it through," said the young woman. "He survived it all. He'll be able to come home now."

Elizabeth nodded and gave the girl a broad smile, but it faded as she looked up at Peter, and images of Joe filled her mind.

As though reading her thoughts, David squeezed her hand and brought her back to the present. "It's over, love," he said.

She nodded. "For now," she said. "For now."

Pooka

Dorothy helped her grandmother down the steps outside the front of the Regal. It was still light, the two of them having attended a matinee. Lizzie was frail, but still determined to get out of the house and live her life. Evening showings were a little much for her, though.

"So, what did you think?" Dorothy asked.

Lizzie shook her head as the two of them walked slowly down the street. "I'm not sure."

"Did you not understand it?"

The older woman flashed a fiery glance at the younger. "Don't be silly, girl. Of course I understood it. I'm just not sure about it."

Dorothy bit her lip. She loved her grandmother but her temper was getting worse as she got older. The loss of both David and Billy had hit her hard and she seemed to find it hard to feel joy.

"I'm not sure that it's a fit subject."

They reached the car, and Dorothy helped Lizzie into the passenger seat. They had finally, the year before, having ganged up on her, managed to get her to agree to stop driving herself.

"Not fit?"

"No, not at all. This is modern films, is it? Is this what they're like?"

Dorothy walked round the car, climbed in behind the wheel, and started the engine. Her grandmother was sitting with her head cocked, waiting for an answer.

"Some of them, I suppose. There are lots of different films."

Lizzie grunted. "Huh, well, I don't think I like them. This whole modern world is just, too much. I don't like it. I'm glad I won't have to put up with it much longer."

"Shush, Grandma. You're not that old."

Lizzie barked a laugh. "I'm eighty years old. That's old enough to start counting the days."

"You have years left, I bet you." Dorothy tried to inject a lighter tone into her voice.

"Oh, I hope not."

After that they were silent on the journey as Dorothy negotiated the traffic in the town centre, and pointed the car for home.

When Lizzie spoke, it was in a low voice, and Dorothy almost missed it. She asked her grandmother to repeat herself.

"I said, 'I have one of those.'"

"One of what?"

Lizzie gave a brittle shrug. "A Harvey. A shadow. A – what did he call it? – Pooka."

Dorothy snatched a glance at her grandmother.

"You do?"

Lizzie gave a laugh, and once it sounded genuine. "No need to look at me like that, my girl. I've not got bats in the belfry yet. I just mean, I feel like I have someone at my side. Always have."

Dorothy thought about this for a moment. Finally, she said, "Joe."

"Nearly sixty years he's been at my shoulder, guiding me, watching out for me."

Dorothy hoped she wouldn't cry. She wouldn't be able to drive if she did.

"I'm just glad he's not alone anymore," Lizzie said softly. "He's got his big brother to look after him now."

They pulled into the driveway, and Dorothy turned to look at her grandmother.

"I love you," she said.

Lizzie looked slightly surprised, and then let out another laugh. "Thank you, sweet girl. I love you too. Same time next week?"

My Grate Grandmother

My grate Grandmother is very very old.

My grate grand mother was born when there was an 18 in the front of the year.

That was called the nineteenth century, even though it has a 18 in front of the year.

My grate grandmother was alive in the first world war and in the second world war.

My grate grandmother has seen a lot of people die. Sometimes she is sad.

My grate grandmother makes cakes for me and my brother.

My brother can not eat many cakes as he is very little. I eat his cakes.

My grate grand mother says that there was no cake in the war, because of rasherning.

I like cake.

My grate grandmother says she remembers when there were no cars.

There are cars everywhere now.

When I grow up I will have a car.

My grate granmother says she remembers when there was no radio or television or movies.

My grate grandmother says she remembers when the lights were gas and not lectric.

My grate grandmother tells storys about when she was young and the queen was called Victoria.

My grate grandmother is very old and I love her very much.

-James, aged 7.

Seeming

It was all going to be new, that was what Edward had been told. It was a new day, a new month, a new year and a new decade. But more than that, it was going to be a new world. It was no longer the fifties. And the forties had been left far behind. Rationing was gone. Austerity was gone. It was a world of colour and possibility.

It was the nineteen sixties and it was going to be a brave new world.

If that was true, then why did Edward feel like he did? Why did he feel that the world was the same as it ever was, and his place was the same as it ever was?

Julia came through into the kitchen to where he was standing at the sink, staring out into the darkened garden.

"Everything alright, love?" she asked him.

He nodded, but didn't turn. He watched his reflection in the mirrored window match its movements to his. He saw her appear over his shoulder. He watched her hand reach out towards his shoulder, and braced for its touch, but she took it back before it made contact, and he felt the sadness of that refusal.

"Everyone was wondering where you had got to," she said.

"I was just cleaning a few glasses," he said, looking down into the soapy water and slipping his hands in, performing the requisite actions. "We were starting to run out."

He glanced up at the window again, and caught her looking at him, and then looking away.

"I think Derek and Jane were thinking of leaving. It is nearly one o'clock."

He heard the catch in her voice when she said Derek's name, and felt his own shoulders stiffen. She knew, that much was obvious. But she would carry on saying nothing. That was clear as well.

"I'll finish these and come through in a moment, then," he said. "To say goodbye."

He watched her nod, and turn away. She paused, and for a moment he thought they were finally going to have the conversation. But instead she started walking again and passed out of his view.

He placed the clean glasses on the drainer and reached for the towel. He rotated the ring on his finger as he dried his hands, and sighed.

The new world, same as the old one.

A Parting

"Peter, take my hand," Lizzie said, turning her wrist to present her palm to him.

He turned in his chair, his knees pressing up against the side of the bed, and he grasped her fingers with his.

"I never thought you would be here, you know. I thought I'd lost you." Her words were sad but her tone was happy.

The others, gathered around the bed, smiled with her.

"I wouldn't be, if it wasn't for you, Mum," he said. "You just wouldn't leave me alone, would you?"

Lizzie raised a weak smile. "No, love, I wouldn't. And I never will."

That reminder of why they had gathered, dulled the mood, and the adults shifted uneasily.

James and Jonathan were also sensitive to the emotion in the room. James, seventeen now, in denim jeans and a white t-shirt, slouched against the door and dug his heels into the carpet. Jonathan, five years his junior, could also feel the tension but was too young to brazen it out. He started crying.

Lizzie, with an effort, lifted her other hand towards him, and he let go of his mother's hand and rushed to the side of the bed. "Be gentle, Jon," Dorothy said to her son, who nodded.

He knelt down and took Lizzie's other hand in his, crying against it. "I don't want you to die, Granny," he said.

She lifted her hand from his and used it to brush the hair from his forehead before letting it drop down to the covers again. "Shush, my boy. I'm ninety five years old. Do you not think I've lived long enough? Do I not get a break?"

"But I'll miss you!" Jonathan wailed. "I don't want you to go."

"Were you raised to be so selfish?" Doris asked. "Why should this be about you?"

"Leave him be, Dor," Edith said to her sister. "He's young. He has to learn."

Doris harrumphed and folded her arms, and Edith smiled at her. She was so much like their mother but would hate to be told so.

"And he will learn," Lizzie said, still aware of what was going on, despite her weakened state. "He will. It'll be hard, but he will. We all will."

"Do you need anything, Mum?" Peter asked.

Lizzie shook her head and looked around at her assembled family: her children, her grandchildren, her great-grandchildren.

"I lived so long," she said. "I've lived so long, and seen so much. I've lost so many people. But look at what I have here. I love you all so much, and I have one thing to be thankful for."

"What's that, Mum?" Peter asked.

"That I got to stay around, and in my right mind, long enough to see you all."

She smiled at them, and looked at each of them in turn, as though fixing them in her mind – taking photographs of them to take with her to wherever she was going.

She gave Peter's hand a little squeeze. "I think I'm going to sleep now."

Peter nodded and let go of her hand. He stood up and the others took that as their cue to file from the room.

Lizzie lived for two more days, and they each sat by her in turn, but that was the last time they were all together. That was what they all remembered.

Being

Eddie sat and nursed his umpteenth cup of tea, and tried to imagine what it would be like to be lost in space. He thought maybe he had a pretty good idea.

It was nearly a year since Julia's passing. His mum had told him, with pride, that there was no history of cancer in their family, but the same could not be said of his wife. She had been just fifty years old, and the shock of the whole thing still hadn't left him.

He sipped his tea and returned his attention to the television where the events unfolding around the moon, the unravelling disaster of Apollo 13, was being played out in sporadic news reports. He paid no attention to the programmes in between the bulletins, but found the small details of the lunar mission to be all consuming.

He imagined himself in the capsule, imagined facing the unending cold and darkness of the universe expanding through the small windows and swallowing him.

He sipped his tea and thought again about the almost full bottle of Julia's pain pills still in the bathroom cabinet.

He sipped his tea, stared at the television set, and lost himself in the vastness of space. And he didn't hear the first knock at the door.

The second, louder, knock roused him from his stupor and he levered himself from the chair and walked through the hallway.

It was either late at night or early in the morning, but he was too far adrift in his thoughts to be concerned about who might be at the door. He opened it and gazed at his visitor.

"Sorry to come round so late, Eddie."

It was Derek.

"Wh–" Eddie's voice caught in his throat and he coughed to clear it.

"Jane's kicked me out," Derek said. "I was hoping I could use your couch for the night. I'll sort something out in the morning."

Eddie nodded and stepped back to let his friend into the house.

The door swung shut and the two men stood face to face in the hallway.

Eddie's brain finally cleared enough to think of asking a question. "She threw you out? Why?"

Derek searched Eddie's eyes, then gave a slight nod. "You know," he said.

Eddie replied with a nod of his own, and took a step forward, closing the space between them. His lips finally pressed against those of the man he had loved for so long and he felt infinity expand.

Diamonds

In the candlelight, all of their faces flickered in and out of existence. Jon took another slug of his beer and laughed again as Billy screamed "Your mother smells of elderberries!" once more.

Then a hand reached out of the darkness, a small square of paper balanced on the end of one finger. It was decorated with small diamonds.

Jon took it and placed it on his tongue, allowing the precious gems to melt.

candle flames flickering in darkness diamonds glittering on black velvet but not yellow flames flickering they look like yellow flames flickering but they are really made from smaller flames gathered together into bright
white

light

light

white

bright

white

light which contains all the light all the colours all the shapes dancing together in the brightness created by power dropping drooping leaving shifting slowing held back by the workers by the miners by the people who hold the power in the palms of their hands and you can see it in the faces as they gather round the flicking diamonds of the candle light each face thinner and slimmer and gaunter than it should be we should be fat and laughing but we're thin and laughing and look at the smiles you can read an entire history in the smile of a friend caught in candlelight and you can read their history you can see the people they have been and the people who came before them you can see generations in the reflection of laughing light in their laughing eyes as they stare at the diamonds spilling from the bright white light of the candle flames illuminating their parents and grandparents and great-grandparents and great-great-grandparents and on and on as they stare out into the new world the new century the new millennium and watch the future approach faster and faster and faster and behind his eyes he can feel the same thing the weight of parents of parents of parents but they have no weight just presence and he can feel them all looking out feeling what he feels and marvelling at a world that has such diamonds in it

Next Turn of the Wheel

"Hi Gramps, how's it going?"

Peter looked away from the television and saw Jimmy approaching across the lounge, snaking round the chairs containing the other inhabitants of the home. He smiled.

Jimmy reached his great-uncle – always known as 'Gramps' to him and his brother – and after a quick hug, careful not to hurt the frail old man, he sat down in the visitor's chair.

Peter smiled at the boy.

"So, how's it going? You're looking well."

Peter didn't respond, but the smile stayed. Jimmy returned it, as best as he could, and looked around the room.

The best way he could have described it was to say that it looked like an old people's home. After all, that's what it was. The framed prints of flowers which adorned the walls were only just discernible against the floral pattern of the wallpaper. Together they clashed nicely with the chintz chairs and the dark swirls of the carpet.

The only things which stood out in the hallucinogenic flora which coated the room, were the inhabitants: beige and lavender silhouettes sporadically interrupting the hectic patterns.

His Gramps was just another one of these, a hunched figure in shades of pastel brown, huddled in the depths of his chair.

Jimmy only came because his mother asked him to. Peter was the head of the family, the last of his generation, but he was no longer really present. His body was still alive, but his mind had already left. Jimmy visited once a month, and his Gramps hadn't spoken to him in over a year. In fact, according to the carers, he hadn't spoken to anyone.

It was no way to go. Jimmy knew the stories about his Gramps and what had happened when he was in the army. An ending like this, as fitting as it might seem, was the last thing he'd have wanted.

He waited the requisite five minutes, alternately talking and smiling at his older relative, and then gathered himself to leave.

"Going already?" asked a voice as he rose. It was a young nurse, one that Jimmy hadn't met before. She was short, with dark hair, and half a smile. Her eyes, though, were stern as they shifted between his face and the coat he held clasped in his hand.

"Well, yeah. He doesn't really know that I'm here."

"Do you think?"

He looked back at his Gramps, then at the nurse

again. "Yeah. He never says anything. Never gives any sign he knows who I am or even that I'm here."

She nodded slowly, and Jimmy could tell that this gesture had nothing to do with agreement.

"You don't see him after you leave, though, do you?" she said.

He shrugged and laughed. "Obviously."

"He's always happier. He eats more food, moves a little quicker, stretches his smile a little wider."

Jimmy looked back at his Gramps. "Really?"

"Really," the nurse replied. "Your visits make a difference, and the longer you stay, the happier he seems. So, why not stay a bit longer. Tell him things. It doesn't matter if he doesn't understand. It's not about you."

Jimmy thought for a moment, then put his jacket back down on the arm of the chair. "You're pretty sharp, aren't you?"

"For a nurse, you mean?"

Jimmy shook his head and treated her to a wide grin. "I mean, for anyone," he replied.

The nurse smiled and ducked her head to hide a blush. Jimmy told her his name.

"Annette," she said, shaking his hand.

"Pleasure to meet you, Annette. Care to join me and my Gramps. I'm sure he'll get a kick out of you."

She shook her head. "Maybe in a bit. I have

rounds to make. Pleasure to meet you too, Jimmy. Maybe I'll see you again."

Jimmy watched her walk away and then turned back to his Gramps. The old man's smile was wider than Jimmy could remember seeing in a long while, and he could almost swear the man was trying to wink at him.

Lives

- There were fourteen of us in the front room, dancing to Mick Jagger and David Bowie. It was strange, like my childhood all over again.
- But they were good, weren't they?
- Honestly, I preferred the original. But then, I was always listening to Motown when you were drooling over Jagger and those guys.
- I thought I'd heard the song before. The Supremes?
- Martha and the Vandellas. Everyone knows that.
- Haha. I wonder what our children would think if they heard us talking like this. We sound like them.
- They think we're too old, too desiccated, to care.
- Maybe we are. I know I'm too old to look after Jonny again.
- Oh no, is he back home.
- Yes. Debbie threw him out. I think it's over for good. I do worry if he'll ever settle down.
- But Jim's okay, isn't he?
- Oh, fine. He and Annette seem like a perfect marriage.

- Well, then.

- No children yet though. They're too happy being just the two of them. I want to tell them they don't have forever, but it's not my place, I have to stay out of it.

- Have you tried dropping hints?

- Of course. I keep track of all his friends from school and mention any of them who have children and how they're getting on.

- Oh, Dotty, that's sneaky!

- I know, Marge, but I have to do something. I want to see some grandchildren before I'm too old to enjoy them.

- You're only sixty, don't be so melodramatic.

- Sixty two, and Jimmy's getting towards forty. Jon's thirty two and back living at home. Where did I go wrong?

- Well, I blame Margaret Thatcher.

- I know you do, Marge. Let's not have that argument again.

- I just wish she had a different name. She's ruined the name Margaret for ever.

- Marge!

- Okay, sorry, sorry. So, did you donate?

- What?

- To the Ethiopians.

- Oh, yes, of course. Terrible business.

- Terrible, yes.

- But it's all a terrible business, really, isn't it?

- What is?

- All of it.

- Dotty, are you okay?

- Oh, ignore me, Marge. Just been a long week what with Jonny moving back in. Get me a cake with the next coffee and I'm sure I'll perk up.

A Second Era

"Do you want some help, Mum?"

"Honestly, Jonathan, how old do you think I am?" She flicked her fingers against his outstretched hand and pulled herself up and out of the car. "If you would just drive something sensible that isn't three inches off the tarmac we wouldn't have any of this trouble, would we?"

Jon stepped back, and Dorothy could hear him counting under his breath. She didn't respond, just turned and closed the door, then started walking towards the hospital.

"Come on, then," she called over her shoulder, and gave a little smile to herself at the irritation this would cause him. It was petty, but she didn't care.

The car park had been busy, so they had had to park some distance away, but Dorothy was moving at speed and they soon reached the entrance. She was scanning the signs when Jon caught up to her.

"Where's the fire?" he asked, out of breath.

She spotted the arrow she was looking for and

set off down a long corridor. She didn't bother to respond. Jon hustled after her.

Three more turnings, each bringing a lengthy walk down identical hallways, and they reached the ward.

Jon had ceased asking questions and just followed along in his mother's wake.

She let him open the heavy fire doors for her and the pair were immediately assaulted by a noise comprising talking, laughing and the cries of new-born children.

"Where will they be?" Jon asked.

Dorothy pointed to a chart on the wall by the nurses' station. It showed the three large rooms which made up the ward with each bed on it marked with a name. She pointed to one of these, and then set off walking again.

There was no crying coming from behind the curtain, just low murmuring. When Dorothy stepped through she found James sitting at the bedside, holding Annette's hand. The new mother looked exhausted and the father didn't look much better. They were talking in low tones so as not to disturb the sleeping bundle in the crib next to them.

The new parents looked up and gave weary smiles. James stood up and hugged Dorothy. "Hi Mum."

Dorothy hugged him back with all her strength, then pushed past to take his seat and squeeze Annette's hand.

"How are you, love?" she asked.

"Tired, but fine."

"And the little one?"

"Gorgeous. Perfect. Asleep."

Dorothy smiled, remembering. "It never gets better than that," she said, and Annette laughed.

"I guess not. Do you want to see her?"

"Don't disturb her."

"No. It's okay. She's due a feed anyway. Jim?"

James moved over from where he had been talking with his brother and reached into the crib, lifting the tiny baby which squirmed a little in his grasp but didn't cry out. He placed the small bundle into his own mother' arms.

Dorothy teased the blanket away from the child's face and peered at it, feeling tears run down her cheeks.

"Beautiful. Just beautiful. Have you picked a name?"

James looked at Annette, who nodded and smiled. "We decided to call her Elizabeth, Mum," he said, "after Granny."

Dorothy nodded, and stroked her finger along little Lizzie's cheek and laughed as the infant's mouth opened, searching.

Communiqué

Der granny   dOT

I loiv you

fromBeth

(Hi Mum, James here. We've been using the new computer to teach Beth her alphabet, and she wanted to send you a message. We told her what letters to hit and she did a pretty good job. Thought we'd send it as she typed it. Adorable, huh?

I hope Jon's managed to get your machine connected so you can read this electronic mail. It's amazing really, that we can send messages so far so easily. It's a brave new world, and all that, as Dad might've said.

Hope you and my bro are okay, and look forward

to seeing you when we come up on the 14th. Take care of each other (and I'll give you a call later, so no need to try and reply!).

Love,
Jimmy.)

Night Flight

Jon was snoring. Dorothy was too excited to sleep. She gazed past him out of the window as the lights of the city below slid past beneath them. The lights in the cabin had been dimmed, but she had a targeted pool of light in her lap illuminating her map. With her finger she was tracing their journey, wanting to know which cities they were passing over, wanting to know where they were and how much closer they were getting to their destination.

"Have you flown before?"

Dorothy turned back to face her questioner. It was a woman in her forties, dressed in a smart black suit and white blouse. She had a sleep mask in her hands and was wringing it between her fingers.

"I'm sorry," said Dorothy, "I've forgotten your name."

"Heather," said the woman. "I'm Heather."

Dorothy nodded. "Yes. Of course. Sorry. No. I've not flown before. I thought this was probably the best time."

"You aren't worried about the Y2K bug?"

Dorothy wrinkled her brow. "I think I heard something about that on the news. Computers, yes?"

"Yes. They said they might all crash at midnight because they reset or something."

Dorothy smiled. "I'm seventy seven years old. I don't care much about computers. My son bought me one years ago, but I mostly just dust it."

The woman leant forward in a conspiratorial fashion. "If they all crash, then things could stop working. They say planes could fall out of the sky!"

Dorothy leaned back in surprise. "Goodness. I can see why you're so worried. And why this one got so drunk." She indicated her snoring son. "But if there's one thing I've learned in life it's that these things are usually blown out of all proportion. I'm sure everything will be fine."

The woman gave a strained smile.

"How long is it until midnight, anyway?" asked Dorothy.

Heather pulled back her sleeve to look at her watch and let out an involuntary, "Oh." She looked up at Dorothy and the older woman could see her visibly relaxing. "It's three minutes past."

"See," said Dorothy, giving her a wide smile. "Happy New Year."

"Happy New Year."

They clunked their plastic cups together.

"Where are you heading, anyway?" asked

Heather when she had taken a long slurp of her drink.

"Australia. I have some distant cousins I've always meant to meet before I die, and I thought while everyone's avoiding flying would be the best time to go."

Heather nodded, and then paused. "You mean you knew about…?"

Dorothy smiled. "I thought you needed to talk about it. Thought it would help."

Heather's face went through contortions as a range of different thoughts and emotions went through her. Finally, she raised her glass again.

"Cheers," she said.

Downstairs, Upstairs

Downstairs

"What on earth is that?" Jimmy asked. He didn't have to shout, not quite, but his voice was raised.

Annette looked up from where she was preparing the dinners – one meal for her, another one entirely for their 'more particular' daughter.

"It's Coldplay, I think," she said, and went back to peeling carrots.

Jimmy grunted. "Is that the same as that Blunt guy? The one who was a soldier?"

His wife stopped what she was doing, turned and looked at him. "Really? How old are you? Eighty? Eighty-five?"

"I'm fifty-seven. You know that," Jimmy grumbled.

"I do, but sometimes you don't half seem a lot older. James Blunt is James Blunt. That," she pointed to the ceiling, "is a band called Coldplay."

Jimmy nodded and carried on unpacking the dishwasher. "All just sounds like whingeing to me," he said.

Annette snorted a laugh. "Well, that I can't argue with. But if you listened to anything recorded after nineteen seventy nine, you might know what it is your daughter's listening to."

Jimmy took a breath to say something, but Annette cut him off. "And don't say there was nothing good recorded after that, because I remember you dancing to plenty of newer music at my sister's last wedding."

James said nothing in response, just carried on slotting cutlery into the spaces in the drawer.

"It's what being a teenager's about now, is it?" he asked, eventually.

""What's that?"

"Sitting in your room, listening to singers whining, and playing on your computer?"

Annette shrugged, stirring the pan absent-mindedly.

"Well, didn't you spend time in your room listening to music and, oh, I don't know, making models or collecting stamps, or dinosaur spotting, or something? You know, back in the old days when everything was in black and white."

She was already squealing before his hands tickled her midriff, and then she was kissing him back, one hand still moving the spoon in the pan.

"She's normal, Jim," Annette said, when they finally gave up their clinch. "She's fine."

He nodded, and squinted up at the ceiling again. "I just wish it was something decent."

Upstairs

Beth clicked on the 'Add friend' button. She didn't know who the person was, but they were a friend of a friend of Cheryl, and they liked some cool music, so they might be cool too. Then she clicked to go back to her main MySpace page to see if anyone had posted anything new.

Her speakers made a 'splink' noise, just audible through the music, and the Messenger icon started flashing. She clicked on it. Sarah had come back and picked up their conversation.

- *so what did you say to hm?* Sarah'd asked.

- I told him that he was cute but was far too old for me, and anyway, I don't date teachers.

- *Hahahahahahahahaha. Lol what did he say?*

- I think he was trying not to laugh, but he wasn't distracted. Gave me detention.

- *o thats crap when for?*

- Next Weds.

- *same as me then that's cool*

- yeah

Beth's phone made a trilling noise and buzzed against her desk. She glanced at the screen. It was a text from Ben.

- BRB, she typed on the computer keyboard, and picked up the phone.

She opened the message and read it quickly, then started typing a reply.

'Not tonight. Got to stay in. Parents! But the weekend?'

She hit 'Send' and put the phone back down. Then she leaned away from the computer and took stock.

Her music was playing – bands that she hated, but that she needed to have listed on MySpace and showing as 'currently playing' on her Messenger window in order to be properly cool – her MySpace was updated, Ben had been fobbed off, and Sarah thought she was both cool and badass. She would have to think of an excuse for why she was no longer in detention when the time came, but that was okay. As if she would actually speak to a teacher like that!

She leaned forward and clicked on the other tab. Her Ancestry.co.uk account was still open, and she looked over the tree which she had created so far. She nodded. She needed to find a few more entries, and then it would be ready for Gran's birthday. She was going to love it.

Then she clicked back to MySpace, and flicked through her Messenger windows. She sighed. It was all such hard work.

After tea, she decided, she would tell everyone that she had said something bad to her mum and her computer privileges had been taken away for the night. Then she could turn it all off, put on some better music and get on with *The Half-Blood Prince*. It was just getting good.

She turned down the volume, and set her status as 'Away'. She'd go and have a chat with the parental units before tea. That'd be good.

Family Again

Jon sat in his usual chair. Jimmy and Annette were on the sofa. Beth stood at the window and looked out on the rain. Dorothy's chair was empty. After the initial pleasantries, silence had fallen. They waited.

"Do you think it freaks her out?" Beth asked, causing the others to start and turn towards her.

"What's that, honey?" Annette asked.

Beth half turned to look back at her family.

"Being alive in the twenty-first. Do you think it freaks her out?"

Annette and Jimmy shook their heads, not quite understanding, but Jon responded. "I think it does, sometimes, yeah. She doesn't say it – not like that anyway – but the way the world works takes her by surprise sometimes. Hell, it shocks me too, so it would be weird if she wasn't, you know, freaked out sometimes."

Beth turned back to the window, and nodded. "Yeah. I guess so. It freaks me out sometimes too."

No one responded to this, and they carried on waiting.

Finally, the sound of slow footsteps in the hallway caused them to turn, and Dorothy appeared in the doorway. She had moved on from her walker to using a stick, and she looked a lot more stable.

"Hello, everyone," she said, and Jimmy and Annette rose to give her a gentle hug and a kiss on the cheek.

"Happy Birthday," they each said.

Dorothy thanked them both and then crooked a finger at Beth who was waiting behind them.

"Can you come with me for a moment?" she asked, then turned to the others. "I won't hold you up much longer, I promise."

The rest of the family settled back, and Beth followed her grandma out of the lounge and into the dining room. The old woman moved over to the dining table, which was covered in papers, picked one off the pile and turned back.

"I've been going through my paperwork, putting affairs in order. I thought, after the fall, it was about time."

Beth wasn't quite sure how to respond, but settled on, "You'll outlive us all, Gran."

The older woman smiled but said nothing. She simply handed the paper to her granddaughter. "Do you remember this?" she asked.

Beth unfolded the large sheet and looked at it. She recognised the handwriting – of course she did, it was hers – and knew exactly what it was.

"Of course," she said.

Dorothy nodded. "Good. Now, when I'm gone, I want you to have it back."

Beth nodded and offered no false protests this time. "Okay. Why?"

Dorothy took the paper and put it back on the table, then she linked her arm through Beth's and steered them back towards the door.

"Because you need to remember the reason you made that for me in the first place: that family is important. And while I'm at the very top – the oldest; the last – you are at the bottom, the only grandchild. So, you need to have it. You need to add to it when the time comes, and pass it on to your children, or grandchildren. It's important to know where you come from. It all counts."

Beth said nothing, just walked with her grandmother back into the lounge. The others all stood, ready to go out for the birthday dinner.

Just before she let go, Dorothy leaned in close to her granddaughter and, in a low voice, said, "And yes, dear. It totally freaks me out. But in a good way."

Through Another Window

Beth sat on the sofa and idly watched the various politicians arguing whether Scotland should vote 'Yes' or 'No' for independence. The referendum was soon, and it was all getting awfully serious. Beth didn't live in Scotland, so couldn't vote, but the whole thing interested her anyway. It was one of those things that only comes along every few hundred years, and she would miss Scotland if they left.

Not that they would actually go anywhere, she mused. They would still be there, north of the border, it was just that the border would be a little more real, she supposed.

She looked down to the screen on her lap and scrolled through her Facebook feed. She laughed at a couple of pictures, aww-ed at the cats, tapped out a few comments on the keyboard, and scrolled on.

Every few moments she glanced down at the clock at the bottom right of the screen. The text had said that her parcel would be delivered between 14.29 and 15.29, but she knew from experience that it was more likely to be the first of those times than the latter.

It wasn't an important delivery. It was a pair of shoes she was fairly sure wouldn't fit, was almost positive wouldn't suit her, and knew for a fact she couldn't afford. She would open the box, try them on, and in a day or two she would send them back.

As the clocked clicked onto twenty five past, she alternated her TV grazing, and her web browsing, with glances through the window. One of the benefits of a ground floor flat was that she could see the delivery arriving; see him arriving.

She didn't need to wonder if it would be him. It always was. That was why she ordered everything from this particular website. They only had one delivery man in the area: Dave, or so the badge on his shirt said.

As the clock ticked over to twenty eight minutes past, she closed the laptop, muted the TV, and stood up. She checked her hair in the mirror over the mantel, and – hanging back in the shadows to avoid being seen from outside – watched through the window.

The clock showing on the News Channel showed 14.30 when the van pulled up outside. She felt her heart start to beat faster in her chest, but held herself back from running to open the door before he even rang the bell.

She watched him walk and down the side of

the house, waited for the chimes, and then walked through.

"Afternoon," he said. "Another little something for you." He smiled and, held out the electronic signature pad for her jerky scrawl. He then swapped that for the box.

She took it off him and, in a moment straight out of a clichéd romcom, their fingers touched. Beth all but gasped.

"Something fun?" Dave asked her, seemingly in no hurry to get to his next appointment.

"Shoes," she said, wishing she could think of something witty to say.

Dave nodded. "Thought so, Right size, right shape. You get to know in this business."

Beth nodded, trying to think of some way to prolong what was turning out to be a rather boring conversation. Then an idea struck her. "Would you like to see them?" she asked.

Dave wrinkled his brow. "What? You want to check they're okay, or something?"

She smiled and shook her head. "No. Do you want to see them? On. Me wearing them?"

Beth was fairly sure that this made Dave blush, and she suddenly had an image of him standing in her bedroom, in his grey uniform, and her in nothing but her new shoes. She held back a giggle and ploughed on. "Tonight, maybe. I could wear them and we could... get a drink?"

Dave's confusion cleared and he nodded.

"You know what?" he said. "I would love to buy your shoes a drink tonight. Eight o'clock, okay?"

Beth nodded.

"Want me to pick you up?" he asked.

"Why not?" she said. "After all, you know where I live."

Afterword

The idea behind writing the 2014 flash collections, of which this is number 7, has to be to find different ways of structuring a collection of flash-fictions such that they stand alone but also hang together.

From the initial inception, the idea of trying to undertake what is often the longest form of novel—the century spanning family saga—in this form, seemed like both a good and a bad idea.

The result is the book you have just read. It is structured so that the first story takes place in 1865 and then each story moves forward 5 years, until we conclude in 2014. In that regard it spans nearly 150 years. It also fills the criteria of following a family. My only concern, now, is whether it contains sufficiently large drama to fit in with most 'sagas'. Perhaps, because this is flash-fiction, I can allow myself to downsize the drama too, to focus on personal, human moments.

However you judge it, I hope you enjoy the book, and the changes it chronicles. A lot of research went into it—from the date at which the British Army changed from red to khaki, to things you would think I should know, like when MySpace was invented—and a lot of effort into making the voice and style appropriate for whatever year the stories are set in. Certainly, and perhaps more than any of the other collections written this year, it has taken a lot of effort and concentration to make sure the details are correct.

And that, as far as I can see, is a good thing. There is no point doing these collections if I'm not stretching myself, is there?

Thanks, as ever, must go to my beta and proof-readers. Specifically thank you to (as ever) my wonderful wife, Kath, and to Diane Simmons and Mark Wise for their assistance.

And thank you too, dear reader, for your persistence with these books. I hope you enjoyed this one, and I'll see you soon for the next.

Until then...

Calum Kerr
Southampton
30-09-14

Other books from **Gumbo Press**:
www.gumbopress.co.uk

28 Far Cries by Marc Nash

This latest collection of flash-fictions from Marc Nash The stories range from the violence of Happy Hour to armoured pole-dancers, from dying superheroes to synesthesia, and from toxic relationships to warlords to the mythic ponderings of incubi and succubi. Each flash-fiction is crafted with Nash's usual close attention to detail and the nuances of language, to captivate and intrigue.

Rapture and what comes after
By Virginia Moffatt

For every tale of everlasting love... You'll find another full of heartbreak and misery Where other love stories end with the coming of the light, Virginia Moffatt goes beyond to show the darkness which can exist in even the happiest relationships. These stories are by turns funny, sad, heart-warming and heart-breaking.

The Book of Small Changes
by Tim Stevenson

This collection takes its inspiration from the Chinese I Ching: where the sea mourns for those it has lost, encyclopaedia salesmen weave their accidental magic, and the only true gift for a king is the silence of snow.

Enough by Valerie O'Riordan

Fake mermaids and conjoined twins, Johannes Gutenberg, airplane sex, anti-terrorism agricultural advice, Bluebeard and more. Ten flash-fictions.

Threshold by David Hartley

Threshold explores the surreal and the strange through thirteen flash-fictions which take us from a neighbour's garden, out into space, and even as far as Preston. But which Preston?

Undead at Heart by Calum Kerr

War of the Worlds meets *The Walking Dead* in this novel from Calum Kerr, author of *31* and *Braking Distance*

The World in a Flash: How to Write Flash-Fiction

by Calum Kerr

A guide for beginners and experienced writers alike to give you insight into the world of flash-fiction. Chapters focus on a range of aspects, with exercises for you to try.

The 2014 Flash365 Collections
by Calum Kerr

Apocalypse

It's the end of the world as we know it. Fire is raining from the sky, monsters are rising from the deep., and the human race is caught in the middle.

The Audacious Adventuress

Our intrepid heroine, Lucy Burkhampton, is orphaned and swindled by her evil nemesis, Lord Diehardt. She must seek a way to prove her right to her family's wealth, to defeat her enemy, and more than anything, to stay alive.

The Grandmaster

Unrelated strangers are being murdered in a brutal fashion. Now it's up to crime-scene cleaner Mike Chambers, with the help of the police, to track down the killer and stop the trail of carnage.

Lunch Hour

One office. Many lives. It is that time of day: the time for poorly-filled, pre-packaged sandwiches; the time to run errands you won't have enough time for; the time to fall in love, to kill or be killed, to take advice from an alien. It's the Lunch Hour.

Time

Time. It's running out. It's flying. It's the most precious thing, and yet it never slows, never stops, never waits. In this collection we visit the past, the future, and sometimes a present we no longer recognise. And it's all about time.

In Conversation with Bob and Jim

Bob and Jim have been friends for forty years, but still have plenty to say to each other - usually accompanied by a libation or two. This collections shines a light on an enduring relationship, the ups and downs, and the prospect of oncoming mortality. It is funny and poignant, and entirely told in dialogue.

Printed in Great Britain
by Amazon

23509356R00067